MW00768751

Hello, Mike!

Aimee Aryal

Illustrated by Danny Moore

MASCOT BOOKS

www.mascotbooks.com

It was a beautiful fall day at
Louisiana State University.

Mike was on his way to Tiger Stadium
to watch a football game.

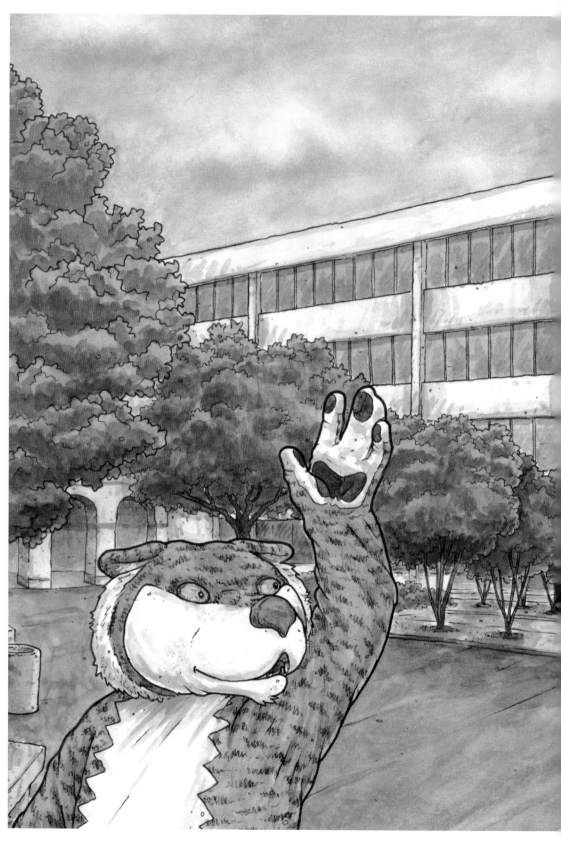

He walked past Middleton Library.

A professor walking by said,
"Hello, Mike!"

Mike walked onto the Quad.

Some students passing by waved,
"Hello, Mike!"

Mike went over to the LSU Union.

A girl running up the steps yelled,
"Hello, Mike!"

Mike passed by the LSU Mounds.

A group of LSU fans stopped
and waved, "Hello, Mike!"

Mike stopped by the Tiger Cage
to see Mike VI. Some alumni
were standing nearby.

The alumni remembered Mike
from their days at LSU.
They said, "Hello, again, Mike!"

Finally, Mike arrived at Tiger Stadium.

As he ran onto the football field,
the crowd cheered, "Geaux, Tigers!"

Mike watched the game from
the sidelines and cheered for the team.

The Tigers scored six points!
The quarterback shouted,
"Touchdown, Mike!"

At halftime the
"Golden Band from Tigerland"
performed on the field.

Mike and the crowd sang,
"Hey Fighting Tigers."

The LSU Tigers
won the football game.

Mike gave the coach a high-five.
The coach said, "Great game, Mike!"

After the football game, Mike was tired.
It had been a long day at
Louisiana State University.

He walked home and climbed into bed.

Goodnight, Mike.

For Anna and Maya, and all of
Mike's little fans. ~ AA

This one is for my parents for being the greatest influences
in my life and always being there. Little Joe and I
couldn't have done it without you. ~ DM

For information please contact Mascot Books,
P.O. Box 220157, Chantilly, VA 20153-0157.

LSU, LOUISIANA STATE UNIVERSITY, LSU TIGERS, FIGHTING TIGERS, BAYOU BENGALS,
and GEAUX TIGERS are trademarks of Louisiana State University and are used under license.

ISBN: 1-932888-00-4

Printed in the United States.

www.mascotbooks.com

Title List

Baseball

Boston Red Sox	Hello, Wally!	Jerry Remy
Boston Red Sox	Wally And His Journey Through Red Sox Nation!	Jerry Remy
Boston Red Sox	Coast to Coast with Wally	Jerry Remy
Boston Red Sox	A Season with Wally	Jerry Remy
Colorado Rockies	Hello, Dinger!	Aimee Aryal
Detroit Tigers	Hello, Paws!	Aimee Aryal
New York Yankees	Let's Go, Yankees!	Yogi Berra
New York Yankees	Yankees Town	Aimee Aryal
New York Mets	Hello, Mr. Met!	Rusty Staub
New York Mets	Mr. Met and his Journey Through the Big Apple	Aimee Aryal
St. Louis Cardinals	Hello, Fredbird!	Ozzie Smith
Philadelphia Phillies	Hello, Phillie Phanatic!	Aimee Aryal
Chicago Cubs	Let's Go, Cubs!	Aimee Aryal
Chicago White Sox	Let's Go, White Sox!	Aimee Aryal
Cleveland Indians	Hello, Slider!	Bob Feller
Seattle Mariners	Hello, Mariner Moose!	Aimee Aryal
Washington Nationals	Hello, Screech!	Aimee Aryal
Milwaukee Brewers	Hello Bernie Brewer!	Aimee Aryal

College

Alabama	Hello, Big Al!	Aimee Aryal
Alabama	Roll Tide!	Ken Stabler
Alabama	Big Al's Journey Through the Yellowhammer State	Aimee Aryal
Arizona	Hello, Wilbur!	Lute Olson
Arkansas	Hello, Big Red!	Aimee Aryal
Arkansas	Big Red's Journey Through the Razorback State	Aimee Aryal
Auburn	Hello, Aubie!	Aimee Aryal
Auburn	War Eagle!	Pat Dye
Auburn	Aubie's Journey Through the Yellowhammer State	Aimee Aryal
Boston College	Hello, Baldwin!	Aimee Aryal
Brigham Young	Hello, Cosmo!	LaVell Edwards
Cal - Berkeley	Hello, Oski!	Aimee Aryal
Clemson	Hello, Tiger!	Aimee Aryal
Clemson	Tiger's Journey Through the Palmetto State	Aimee Aryal
Colorado	Hello, Ralphie!	Aimee Aryal
Connecticut	Hello, Jonathan!	Aimee Aryal
Duke	Hello, Blue Devil!	Aimee Aryal
Florida	Hello, Albert!	Aimee Aryal
Florida	Albert's Journey Through the Sunshine State	Aimee Aryal
Florida State	Let's Go, 'Noles!	Aimee Aryal
Georgia	Hello, Hairy Dawg!	Aimee Aryal
Georgia	How 'Bout Them Dawgs!	Vince Dooley
Georgia	Hairy Dawg's Journey Through the Peach State	Vince Dooley
Georgia Tech	Hello, Buzz!	Aimee Aryal
Gonzaga	Spike, The Gonzaga Bulldog	Mike Pringle
Illinois	Let's Go, Illini!	Aimee Aryal
Indiana	Let's Go, Hoosiers!	Aimee Aryal
Iowa	Hello, Herky!	Aimee Aryal
Iowa State	Hello, Cy!	Amy DeLashmutt
James Madison	Hello, Duke Dog!	Aimee Aryal
Kansas	Hello, Big Jay!	Aimee Aryal
Kansas State	Hello, Willie!	Dan Walter
Kentucky	Hello, Wildcat!	Aimee Aryal
LSU	Hello, Mike!	Aimee Aryal
LSU	Mike's Journey Through the Bayou State	Aimee Aryal
Maryland	Hello, Testudo!	Aimee Aryal
Michigan	Let's Go, Blue!	Aimee Aryal
Michigan State	Hello, Sparty!	Aimee Aryal
Minnesota	Hello, Goldy!	Aimee Aryal
Mississippi	Hello, Colonel Rebel!	Aimee Aryal

Pro Football

Carolina Panthers	Let's Go, Panthers!	Aimee Aryal
Chicago Bears	Let's Go, Bears!	Aimee Aryal
Dallas Cowboys	How 'Bout Them Cowboys!	Aimee Aryal
Green Bay Packers	Go, Pack, Go!	Aimee Aryal
Kansas City Chiefs	Let's Go, Chiefs!	Aimee Aryal
Minnesota Vikings	Let's Go, Vikings!	Aimee Aryal
New York Giants	Let's Go, Giants!	Aimee Aryal
New York Jets	J-E-T-S! Jets, Jets, Jets!	Aimee Aryal
New England Patriots	Let's Go, Patriots!	Aimee Aryal
Seattle Seahawks	Let's Go, Seahawks!	Aimee Aryal
Washington Redskins	Hail To The Redskins!	Aimee Aryal

Basketball

Dallas Mavericks	Let's Go, Mavs!	Mark Cuban
Boston Celtics	Let's Go, Celtics!	Aimee Aryal

Other

Kentucky Derby	White Diamond Runs For The Roses	Aimee Aryal
Marine Corps Marathon	Run, Miles, Run!	Aimee Aryal
Mississippi State	Hello, Bully!	Aimee Aryal
Missouri	Hello, Truman!	Todd Donoho
Nebraska	Hello, Herbie Husker!	Aimee Aryal
North Carolina	Hello, Rameses!	Aimee Aryal
North Carolina	Rameses' Journey Through the Tar Heel State	Aimee Aryal
North Carolina St.	Hello, Mr. Wuf!	Aimee Aryal
North Carolina St.	Mr. Wuf's Journey Through North Carolina	Aimee Aryal
Notre Dame	Let's Go, Irish!	Aimee Aryal
Ohio State	Hello, Brutus!	Aimee Aryal
Ohio State	Brutus' Journey	Aimee Aryal
Oklahoma	Let's Go, Sooners!	Aimee Aryal
Oklahoma State	Hello, Pistol Pete!	Aimee Aryal
Oregon	Let's Go Ducks!	Aimee Aryal
Oregon State	Hello, Benny the Beaver!	Aimee Aryal
Penn State	Hello, Nittany Lion!	Aimee Aryal
Penn State	We Are Penn State!	Joe Paterno
Purdue	Hello, Purdue Pete!	Aimee Aryal
Rutgers	Hello, Scarlet Knight!	Aimee Aryal
South Carolina	Hello, Cocky!	Aimee Aryal
South Carolina	Cocky's Journey Through the Palmetto State	Aimee Aryal
So. California	Hello, Tommy Trojan!	Aimee Aryal
Syracuse	Hello, Otto!	Aimee Aryal
Tennessee	Hello, Smokey!	Aimee Aryal
Tennessee	Smokey's Journey Through the Volunteer State	Aimee Aryal
Texas	Hello, Hook 'Em!	Aimee Aryal
Texas	Hook 'Em's Journey Through the Lone Star State	Aimee Aryal
Texas A & M	Howdy, Reveille!	Aimee Aryal
Texas A & M	Reveille's Journey Through the Lone Star State	Aimee Aryal
Texas Tech	Hello, Masked Rider!	Aimee Aryal
UCLA	Hello, Joe Bruin!	Aimee Aryal
Virginia	Hello, CavMan!	Aimee Aryal
Virginia Tech	Hello, Hokie Bird!	Aimee Aryal
Virginia Tech	Yea, It's Hokie Game Day!	Frank Beamer
Virginia Tech	Hokie Bird's Journey Through Virginia	Aimee Aryal
Wake Forest	Hello, Demon Deacon!	Aimee Aryal
Washington	Hello, Harry the Husky!	Aimee Aryal
Washington State	Hello, Butch!	Aimee Aryal
West Virginia	Hello, Mountaineer!	Aimee Aryal
Wisconsin	Hello, Bucky!	Aimee Aryal
Wisconsin	Bucky's Journey Through the Badger State	Aimee Aryal

Order online at **mascotbooks.com** using promo code " **free**" to receive **FREE SHIPPING!**

More great titles coming soon!

info@mascotbooks.com

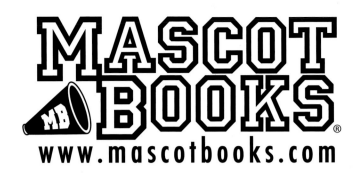
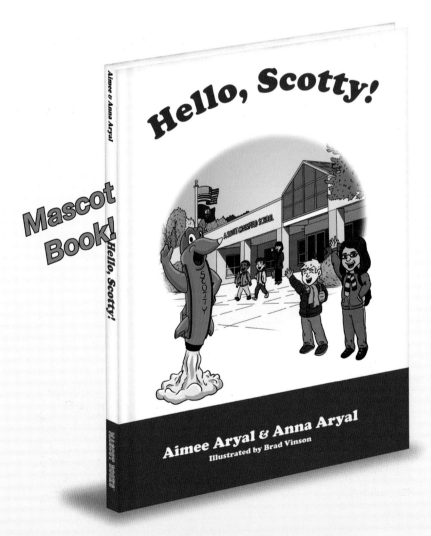